Leaves

David Ezra Stein

SCHOLASTIC INC.
New York Toronto London Auckland Sydney
Mexico City New Delhi Hong Kong Buenos Aires

ISBN-13: 978-0-545-10718-1
ISBN-10: 0-545-10718-0

Copyright © 2007 by David Ezra Stein. All rights reserved.
Published by Scholastic Inc., 557 Broadway, New York, NY 10012, by arrangement with G. P. Putnam's Sons, a division of Penguin Young Readers Group, a member of Penguin Group (USA) Inc. SCHOLASTIC and associated logos are trademarks and/or registered trademarks of Scholastic Inc.

12 11 10 9 8 7 6 5 4 3 2 1   8 9 10 11 12 13/0

Printed in the U.S.A.   40

First Scholastic printing, September 2008

Design by Gunta Alexander
Text set in Green
The art was created with bamboo pen and watercolors.

For my mother,
a bear of great heart
and an exceptional human being.

It was his first year.

Everything

was going well

until the first leaf fell.

"Are you okay?" he wondered.

Then . . . a red one fell,
a yellow one fell,

all over his island, the leaves
were falling.

He tried to catch them
and put them back on . . .

but it was not the same.

He sat beneath a tree
and watched them go, all around.

But he grew sleepy,

and so . . .

he found a hole

and filled it with leaves,

and went to sleep,

just as the wind began to blow.

Winter came.

He slept, snug in the ground,

while the snow piled thick.

In the spring,

with wide eyes, he woke.

He felt the sun

and saw the little buds on the bare arms of the trees

and the tiny leaves that had begun to unfold.

"Welcome!" he cried.

And, he thought, the leaves welcomed him.